(7)

KT-436-576

263752

The Emperor Who Hated Yellow

To Mandy and Owen

★ ★ ★ ★

BAREFOOT BEGINNERS
an imprint of
Barefoot Books
PO Box 95
Kingswood
Bristol BS30 5BH

Text and illustrations copyright © 1996 by Jim Edmiston
The moral right of Jim Edmiston to be identified
as the author and illustrator of this work has been asserted.

First published in Great Britain in 1996 by Barefoot Books Ltd. All rights reserved.
No part of this book may be reproduced in any form or by any means, electronic or mechanical,
including photocopying, recording, or by any information storage and retrieval system, without
permission in writing from the publisher. British Library Cataloguing-in-Publication Data: a catalogue
record for this book is available from the British Library.

Paperback ISBN 1 898000 23 9

Graphic design by Design/Section, Frome
Colour reproduction by Grafiscan, Verona
Printed in Singapore by Tien Wah Press (Pte) Ltd.

3 5 7 9 8 6 4

FALKIRK COUNCIL
LIBRARY SUPPORT
FOR SCHOOLS

The Emperor Who Hated Yellow

Written and illustrated by Jim Edmiston

BAREFOOT BOOKS

BATH

The Emperor stood in front of his mirror. 'Mm,' he said, 'the longest beard in the world.' It was so long, sometimes he tripped over it.

His beloved cat, Mustard, stood in front of the mirror too. He crinkled his crinkly whiskers, twitched his tail and purred.

The Emperor admired his fat tummy. He gave it a friendly pat. 'Yes,' he said, 'the roundest tummy in the world.' It was so fat and round, Mustard loved to curl up and fall asleep on it.

The Emperor liked nothing better than to sit on his big blue throne and stroke Mustard. 'You are the best cat in the world,' whispered the Emperor. Mustard closed his eyes and purred.

The Emperor was very happy until, one day, Mustard disappeared. This made the Emperor very bad-tempered. He ordered his servants

to search the whole palace, but although they looked in every nook and cranny they could not find Mustard anywhere. Can you find him?

From then on, the Emperor hated yellow. He did not want to be reminded of losing Mustard. 'I hate anything yellow!' he cried. He never wore anything the slightest bit yellow. If he was given yellow

socks or boxer shorts for Christmas, they went straight into the bin. He stamped his feet. Every day, he searched the palace but still he could not find Mustard. Can you find him?

The Emperor refused to eat scrambled eggs or cheese, lemon or pineapple juice, grapefruit or custard, and especially not mustard sandwiches. He had always liked bananas, but now he fumed, 'Take

those horrible things away, and paint them purple with orange spots!'
And he shouted, 'If you want to bring me anything yellow, bring me
my cat Mustard!' But no-one could find Mustard. Can you find him?

The Emperor stopped using a yellow sponge and lemon soap in his bath.
He used to enjoy bursting the bubbles, but it was no fun anymore.

He didn't even feel like playing with his red sail-boat. He could think of nothing else except where his cat had gone. Can you see Mustard?

At bedtime, his servants brought the Emperor his white teddy bear, blue cuddly blanket and red hot water bottle. 'Draw the curtains!' he shouted. 'Blow out the candles! Leave me alone! I don't want to see

the moon or the stars! I only want to see my yellow cat Mustard!' But
even in his dreams, the poor Emperor couldn't see him anywhere.
Can you?

The Emperor thought the sun was far too yellow. He only walked in his garden on cloudy days. Buttercups kept out of his way. Daffodils grew in secret corners. Canaries sang from leafy, dark trees.

At the bottom of the garden, there was a thick jungle. It growled with rare, green leopards and turquoise tigers. Somewhere, a cat purred. The Emperor couldn't hear or see him, but the flowers could. Can you?

One morning, the Emperor was combing his long beard and patting his
round, fat tummy. The door opened. In came his youngest grandchild.
She was wearing a yellow jersey, yellow trousers and yellow shoes.

Her name was Saffron, and she was pulling a yellow, wooden duck on wheels. 'Where's Mustard?' asked Saffron. 'My duck wants to play with him.' Can you see Mustard?

'I can't stand yellow!' shouted the Emperor. He snorted and fumed.
He pulled at his beard. He called for his servants, but they were too
busy removing the lemon from the lemon meringue pie, and shoo-ing

some swallowtail butterflies out of the garden. He shouted and shouted, but everyone else was painting the bananas. Everyone except Mustard. Do you know where he is hiding?

So the Emperor chased Saffron round the room. She just giggled.
'Quack, quack!' went the yellow, wooden duck behind her. He chased
her along corridors, round corners, and up winding stairs, until they

were in the highest tower of the palace. But the Emperor's long beard and fat tummy slowed him down. He was far too flustered to notice Mustard. Can you find him?

Saffron hid at the top of the tower on a high balcony. When the Emperor stopped panting, he could hear a wooden quacking noise. He rushed out, but tripped over his beard and fell over the edge.

Down and down he tumbled. Down and down. Everyone watched with horror as he fell. He was sure to land with an enormous bump. Can you see Mustard watch him fall?

But, just in time, a hundred yellow canaries flew up and caught hold of his long black beard. And, flapping their tiny wings, they slowly and

carefully lowered him to the ground. There, they gently laid him in a bed
of bright, yellow daffodils. The Emperor was saved! But best of all …

… there, among the daffodils, was Mustard. Up above, the sun shone
happily. The Emperor smiled his biggest smile. He stroked the longest

beard in the world, patted the roundest tummy, and hugged the
yellowest cat you have ever seen.

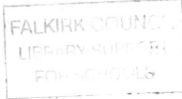

FALKIRK COUNCIL
LIBRARY SUPPORT
FOR SCHOOLS

JIM EDMISTON is a maker of colourful wooden toys in Bath, Somerset. While the characters in this book are not based on any of his toys, the style and use of colour is the same. For more information about his toymaking, contact Jim by telephone on 01225 331909, fax on 01225 331927, or e-mail at Jim Toys@aol.com.